Reddy Fox sprang up as if someone had stuck a pin into him. FRONTISPIECE. *See page 5.*

DOVER
CHILDREN'S THRIFT CLASSICS

The Adventures of Unc' Billy Possum

THORNTON W. BURGESS

Original Illustrations by Harrison Cady
Adapted by Pat Stewart

PUBLISHED IN ASSOCIATION WITH THE
THORNTON W. BURGESS MUSEUM AND THE
GREEN BRIAR NATURE CENTER, SANDWICH, MASSACHUSETTS,
BY
DOVER PUBLICATIONS, INC., MINEOLA, NEW YORK

DOVER CHILDREN'S THRIFT CLASSICS
EDITOR OF THIS VOLUME: JANET BAINE KOPITO

Bibliographical Note

This Dover edition, first published in 2003 in association with the Thornton W. Burgess Museum and the Green Briar Nature Center, Sandwich, Massachusetts, who have provided a new introduction, is an unabridged republication of the work first published by Little, Brown, and Company, Boston, in 1914. The original Harrison Cady illustrations have been adapted for this new edition by Pat Stewart.

Library of Congress Cataloging-in-Publication Data

Burgess, Thornton W. (Thornton Waldo), 1874–1965.
    The adventures of Unc' Billy Possum / Thornton W. Burgess ; original illustrations by Harrison Cady, adapted by Pat Stewart.
        p. cm. — (Dover children's thrift classics)
    "Published in association with the Thornton W. Burgess Museum and the Green Briar Nature Center, Sandwich, Massachusetts."
    "An unabridged republication of the work first published by Little, Brown, and Company, Boston, in 1914"—Verso t.p.
    Summary: When Unc' Billy Possum plans to bring his family to join him in the Green Forest, some of the animals look forward to welcoming them, others look forward to causing trouble, and Unc' Billy himself has an adventure in Farmer Brown's hen-house.
    ISBN 0-486-43031-6 (pbk.)
    [1. Opossums—Fiction. 2. Animals—Fiction.] I. Title: Adventures of Uncle Billy Possum. II. Cady, Harrison, 1877– ill. III. Stewart, Pat Ronson, ill. IV. Title. V. Series.

PZ7.B917Aj 2003
[Fic]—dc22

                2003053259

Manufactured in the United States of America
Dover Publications, Inc., 31 East 2nd Street, Mineola, N.Y. 11501

Introduction to the Dover Edition

Unc' Billy Possum liked living in the Green Forest and always enjoyed visiting with his neighbors, but something was bothering him: he was lonely! When Unc' Billy first moved to the Green Forest, he had left all his family back in "Ol' Virginny." He missed his family so much that he decided to move them from "down south." Peter Rabbit had a wonderful idea of planning a surprise party to welcome Unc' Billy's family to the Green Forest. Unfortunately, Sammy Jay, Reddy Fox, Shadow the Weasel, and Blacky the Crow had plans to spoil the party.

As you read *The Adventures of Unc' Billy Possum*, you will learn how Old Mr. Toad saved the day, and had a few surprises of his own. The story of Unc' Billy Possum is one of the Adventures Series books written by author and naturalist Thornton W. Burgess. It was published in 1914. Mr. Burgess was a well-known children's author who wrote over 170 different children's books. He also wrote a syndicated newspaper column that appeared in newspapers all across the country for over fifty years.

Thornton Burgess was born in 1874 in Sandwich, Massachusetts, on Cape Cod. Mr. Burgess was

a firm believer that "Nature was the universal teacher." For over a quarter of a century, the Thornton W. Burgess Society has followed his example by providing environmental education programs to children all across Cape Cod. Each year, over 30,000 people visit the Society's two facilities, the Thornton W. Burgess Museum and the Green Briar Nature Center in Sandwich, where they learn more about Thornton Burgess, his wonderful tales of nature, and, especially, the animals that live in the Green Forest and Green Meadow. You can learn more about the Thornton W. Burgess Society at its website: **www.thorntonburgess.org**.

Contents

List of Illustrations

The Adventures of
Unc' Billy Possum

I
Unc' Billy Possum Is Caught

THE Green Meadows were thrown into great excitement late one afternoon, just as the black shadows came creeping down from the Purple Hills. Reddy Fox brought the news, and when he told it he grinned as if he enjoyed it and was glad of it.

"Old Billy Possum is dead. I know it because I saw Farmer Brown's boy carrying him home by the tail," said Reddy. "So you see he wasn't so smart as you thought he was," he added maliciously.

No one really believed Reddy Fox, for every one knows that he seldom tells the truth, but when Jimmy Skunk came mournfully down the Crooked Little Path and said that it was true, they had to believe it. Then everybody began to talk about Unc' Billy and say nice things about him and tell how much they had enjoyed having him live in the Green Forest since he came up from "Ol' Virginny." That is, everybody but Reddy Fox said so. Reddy said that it served Unc' Billy right, because he was of no account, anyway. Then everybody began to hoot and hiss at Reddy until he was glad enough to slink away.

And while they were all saying such nice things

1

about him, Unc' Billy Possum was having an exciting adventure. For once he had been too bold. He had gone up to Farmer Brown's hen-house before dark. Jimmy Skunk had tried to stop him, but he had heeded Jimmy Skunk not at all. He had said that he was hungry and wanted an egg, and he couldn't wait till dark to get it. So off he had started, for Unc' Billy Possum is very headstrong and obstinate.

He had reached the hen-house and slipped inside without being seen. The nests were full of eggs, and soon Unc' Billy was enjoying his feast so that he forgot to keep watch. Suddenly the door opened, and in stepped Farmer Brown's boy to get some eggs for supper. There was no time to run. Unc' Billy just dropped right down in his tracks as if he were dead.

When Farmer Brown's boy saw him, he didn't know what to make of him, for he had never seen Unc' Billy before.

"Well, well, I wonder what happened to this fellow," said Farmer Brown's boy, turning Unc' Billy over with the toe of one foot. "He certainly is dead enough, whatever killed him. I wonder what he was doing in here."

Then he saw some egg on Unc' Billy's lips. "Ho! ho!" shouted Farmer Brown's boy. "So you are the thief who has been getting my eggs!" And picking up Unc' Billy by the tail, he started with him for the house.

As they passed the woodpile, he tossed Unc' Billy on the chopping-block while he gathered an armful of kindlings to take to the house. When he turned to pick up Unc' Billy again, Unc' Billy wasn't there.

Farmer Brown's boy dropped his wood and hunted everywhere, but not a trace of Unc' Billy could he find.

II
Reddy Fox Thinks He Sees a Ghost

REDDY Fox came down the Lone Little Path through the Green Forest on his way to the Green Meadows. He had brushed his red coat until it shone. His white waistcoat was spotless, and he carried his big tail high in the air, that it might not become soiled. Reddy was feeling as fine as he looked. He would have liked to sing, but every time he tried his voice cracked, and he was afraid that some one would hear him and laugh at him. If there is one thing that Reddy Fox dislikes more than another, it is being laughed at.

Reddy chuckled at his thoughts, and what do you think he was thinking about? Why, about how he had seen Farmer Brown's boy carrying off Unc' Billy Possum by the tail the afternoon before. He knew how Farmer Brown's boy had caught Unc' Billy in the hen-house, and with his own eyes he had seen Unc' Billy carried off. Of course Unc' Billy was dead. There could be no doubt about it. And Reddy was glad of it. Yes, Sir, Reddy was glad of it. Unc' Billy Possum had made altogether too many friends in the Green Forest and on the Green Meadows, and he had made Reddy the laughing-stock of them all by the way he had dared Reddy to meet

4

Bowser the Hound, and actually had waited for Bowser while Reddy ran away.

Reddy remembered that Unc' Billy's hollow tree was not far away. He would go over that way, just to have another look at it. So over he went. There stood the old hollow tree, and half way up was the door out of which Unc' Billy used to look down on him and grin. It was Reddy's turn to grin now. Presently he sat down with his back against the foot of the tree, crossed his legs, looked this way and that way to make sure that no one was about, and then in a dreadfully cracked voice he began to sing:

> "Ol' Bill Possum, he's gone before!
>   Ol' Bill Possum, he is no more!
>   Bill was a scamp, Sir;
>   Bill was a thief!
>   Bill stole an egg, Sir;
>   Bill came to grief.
>   Ol' Bill Possum, it served him right;
>   And he is no more, for he died last night."

"Very good, Sah, very good. Ah cert'nly am obliged to yo'all for yo' serenade," said a voice that seemed to come out of the tree at Reddy's back.

Reddy Fox sprang up as if some one had stuck a pin into him. Every hair stood on end, as he looked up at Unc' Billy's doorway. Then his teeth began to chatter with fright. Looking out of Unc' Billy's doorway and grinning down at him was something that looked for all the world like Unc' Billy himself.

"It must be his ghost!" said Reddy, and tucking his tail between his legs, he started up the Crooked Little Path as fast as his legs could take him.

Reddy never once looked back. If he had, he might have seen Unc' Billy Possum climb down from the hollow tree and shake hands with Jimmy Skunk, who had just come along.

"How did Ah do it? Why, Ah just pretended Ah was daid, when Farmer Brown's boy caught me," explained Unc' Billy. "Of course he wouldn't kill a daid Possum. So when he tossed me down on the chopping-block and turned his back, Ah just naturally came to life again, and here Ah am."

Unc' Billy Possum grinned broader than ever, and Jimmy Skunk grinned, too.

III
Unc' Billy Possum Sends for His Family

THE news that Unc' Billy Possum wasn't dead at all but was back in his hollow tree in the Green Forest soon spread through all the Green Forest and over the Green Meadows. Everybody hastened to pay their respects, that is everybody but Reddy Fox. Unc' Billy and his partner, Jimmy Skunk, told every one who called how Reddy Fox had thought that Unc' Billy was a ghost and had been frightened almost to death, so that he ran away as fast as his legs could take him. Unc' Billy grinned as he told how Reddy had sat under the hollow tree and tried to sing because he was so glad that Unc' Billy was dead, and all the little people of the Green Forest and the Green Meadows laughed until their sides ached when in a funny, cracked voice Unc' Billy sang the song for them.

Thereafter whenever one of them caught sight of Reddy Fox at a safe distance, he would shout:

"Ol' Bill Possum, he's gone before!
Ol' Bill Possum, he is no more!"

It got so that Reddy never came down on the Green Meadows in the daytime, and at night he avoided meeting any one if possible, even his old friend,

7

Bobby Coon. And of course Reddy Fox hated Unc' Billy Possum more than ever.

But Unc' Billy didn't care, not he! He knew that all the rest of the little people of the Green Forest and the Green Meadows thought him the smartest of them all, because of the way in which he had fooled Bowser the Hound and Farmer Brown's boy. He liked his neighbors, he liked the Green Forest, and so he made up his mind that this was the place for him to stay.

But in spite of all his friends, Unc' Billy was lonesome. The longer he stayed, the more lonesome he grew. Unc' Billy wanted his family, whom he had left way down in "Ol' Virginny." Finally he told Jimmy Skunk all about it, and for once Unc' Billy had forgotten how to grin. Yes, Sir, Unc' Billy had forgotten how to grin. Instead he just wept, wept great big tears of lonesomeness.

"Ah reckon Ah'll have to go back to Ol' Virginny, Ah cert'nly do," said Unc' Billy Possum.

Jimmy Skunk grew very thoughtful. Since he and Unc' Billy Possum had been in partnership, Jimmy had had more eggs to eat than ever before in his whole life. Now Unc' Billy was talking about going away. Jimmy thought very hard. Then he had a bright idea.

"Why not send for your family to come here and live in the Green Forest, Uncle Billy?" he asked.

Unc' Billy stopped crying. His two little eyes

looked up sharply. "How do yo'all reckon Ah can send word?" he asked.

Jimmy scratched his head. "There's Mr. Skimmer the Swallow; he's fixing to go South. Perhaps he'll take the message to your family," said he.

"The very thing!" cried Unc' Billy Possum, wiping his eyes. "Ah thanks yo', Sah. Ah does, indeed. Ah'll see Mistah Skimmer at once."

And without another word Unc' Billy Possum started down the Crooked Little Path for the Green Meadows to look for Skimmer the Swallow.

IV

Bobby Coon Enters the Wrong House

AFTER Unc' Billy Possum had arranged with Skimmer the Swallow, who was going South, to take a message to his family in "Ol' Virginny," telling them to come and join him in the Green Forest, he at once began to make preparations to receive them. Unc' Billy isn't any too fond of work. He had a lot rather that some one else should do the work for him, and he is smart enough to fix it so that usually some one else does.

But getting ready to receive his family was different. No one else could arrange things to suit him. This was Unc' Billy's own job, and he tended right to it every minute of the day. First of all he had to clean house. He had been keeping bachelor's hall so long in the big hollow tree that things were not very tidy. So Unc' Billy cleaned house, and while he worked he whistled and sang. Peter Rabbit, passing that way, overheard Unc' Billy singing:

"Mah ol' woman is away down Souf—
    Come along! Come along!
Ain't nothin' sharper than the tongue in her mouf—
    Come along! Come along!
She once was pretty, but she ain't no mo',

10

But she cooks mah meals an' she sweeps mah flo';
She darns mah stockings an' she mends mah coat,
An' she knows jes' how mah chillun fer to tote—
    Come along! Come along!

"Mah pickaninnies am a-headin' dis way—
    Come along! Come along!
Daddy am a-watchin' fo' 'em day by day—
    Come along! Come along!
Mah ol' haid aches when Ah thinks ob de noise
De's boun' to be wid dem gals an' boys,
But Ah doan care if it busts in two
If de good Lord brings dem chillun troo—
    Come along! Come along!"

Every little while Unc' Billy Possum would sit down to rest, for he wasn't used to so much real work. But finally he got his house clean and made as comfortable as possible, and about that time he began to think how good an egg would taste. The more he thought about it, the more he wanted that egg.

"It's no use talking, Ah just naturally has to have that egg," said Unc' Billy to himself, and off he started for Farmer Brown's.

Now Unc' Billy was hardly out of sight when along came Bobby Coon. Bobby Coon was absent-minded, or else he was so sleepy that he didn't know what he was doing, for Bobby Coon had been out all night. Anyway, when he reached Unc' Billy Possum's hollow tree, he began to climb up it just as if it were his own. He looked in at Unc' Billy's door. There was the most comfortable bed that he had seen for a long time. He looked this way and he looked that way. Nobody was in sight. Then he looked in at Unc' Billy's door once more. That bed certainly did look soft and comfortable. Bobby Coon chuckled to himself.

"I believe I'll just see if that bed is as comfortable as it looks," said he.

And two minutes later Bobby Coon was curled up fast asleep in Unc' Billy Possum's bed.

V
Bobby Coon Is Waked Up

"Dey's a-coming, dey's a-coming, dey's a-coming mighty
    soon,
    But dey can't come soon enuff fo' me!
Dey's a-coming, dey's a-coming at de turning ob de
    moon,
    Whar Ah waits in mah ol' holler tree!"

UNC' Billy Possum was singing to himself, as he
slowly trudged home from Farmer Brown's
hen-house. He was feeling very good, very good
indeed, was Unc' Billy Possum. No one appreciates
strictly fresh eggs more than Unc' Billy does, and
he had found more than he could eat waiting for
him in Farmer Brown's hen-house. Now his stomach was full, his house had been cleaned and put
to rights, ready for his family when they should
arrive from "Ol' Virginny," and he had nothing to
do but wait for them. So he trudged along and sang
in a funny, cracked voice.

Presently he came to his big hollow tree and
started to climb up to the door of his house. Half
way up he broke off short in the middle of his song
and sat down on a convenient branch. He put one
ear against the trunk of the tree and listened. Then
he put the other ear against the tree and listened.

There certainly was a funny noise, and it seemed to come from right inside his hollow tree. Unc' Billy turned and looked up at his doorway, scratching his head thoughtfully with one hand.

"Mah goodness!" said Unc' Billy, "it cert'nly sounds like there was somebody in mah house!"

Then very softly Unc' Billy crept up to his doorway and peeped in. It was dark inside, so that Unc' Billy could see little else than that his nice, freshly made, comfortable bed was all mussed up. But if he couldn't see, he could hear. Oh, yes, indeed, Unc' Billy could hear perfectly well, and what he heard was a snore! There was some one in Unc' Billy's house, and more than that, they were fast asleep in Unc' Billy's bed.

"Mah goodness! Mah goodness!" exclaimed Unc' Billy Possum, and his two sharp little eyes began to snap. Then he stuck his head in at the door and shouted:

"Hi, yo'all! What yo' doing in mah house?"

The only answer was another snore. Unc' Billy waited a minute. Then he put his head in once more.

"Yo' better come out of mah house, Mr. Who-ever-yo'-are, before Ah comes in and puts yo' out!" shouted Unc' Billy.

The only answer was a snore louder than before. Then Unc' Billy quite lost his temper. Some one who had no business there was in his house! He didn't know who it was, and he didn't care. They

My! my! my! Such a rumpus as there was right away
in that hollow tree! *See page 16.*

were going to come out or he would know why not. Unc' Billy gritted his teeth and in he went.

My! my! my! such a rumpus as there was right away in that hollow tree! Peter Rabbit happened to be coming along that way and heard it. Peter stopped and gazed at the hollow tree with eyes and mouth wide open. Such a snarling and growling! Then out of the doorway began to fly leaves and moss. They were part of Unc' Billy's bed. Then Peter saw a big ringed tail hanging out of the doorway. Peter recognized it right away. No one possessed a tail like that but Bobby Coon.

In a minute Bobby followed his tail, hastily backing down the tree. Then Unc' Billy's sharp little old face appeared at the doorway. Unc' Billy looked down at Peter Rabbit and grinned.

"Ah guess Mistah Coon done make a mistake when he went to bed in mah house," said he.

And Bobby Coon sheepishly admitted that he did.

VI
Sammy Jay Learns Peter Rabbit's Secret

"I'm Mr. Jaybird, tee-hee-hee!
I'm Mr. Jaybird; you watch me!
You've got to rise 'fore break of day
If you want to fool old Mr. Jay."

OVER and over Sammy Jay hummed this, as he brushed his handsome blue and white coat. Then he laughed as he remarked to no one in particular, for no one was near enough to hear: "Peter Rabbit's got a secret. When Peter goes about whispering, it's a sure sign that he's got a secret. He thinks that he can keep it from me, but he can't. Oh, my, no! I never knew of a secret that could be kept by more than two people, and already I've seen Peter whisper to five. I'll just see what Reddy Fox knows about it."

With a flirt of his tail Sammy Jay started for the Green Meadows, where Reddy Fox was busy hunting for his breakfast.

"It's a fine morning, Reddy Fox," said Sammy Jay.

"It would be finer, if I could fill my stomach faster," replied Reddy.

"That's a pretty good secret of Peter Rabbit's, isn't it?" asked Sammy, pretending to look very wise.

17

Reddy pricked up his sharp little ears. "What secret?" he demanded.

"If you don't know, I'm not going to tell," retorted Sammy Jay, just as if he knew all about it, and off he flew to hunt up his cousin, Blacky the Crow. Blacky knew nothing about Peter Rabbit's secret, nor did Shadow the Weasel, whom he met by the way. But Sammy Jay was not in the least bit discouraged.

"I'll try Johnny Chuck; he'll know," said Sammy to himself.

He found Johnny sitting on his doorstep, watching the world go by.

"Good morning, Johnny Chuck," said Sammy, with a low bow.

"Good morning," replied Johnny Chuck, who always is polite.

"Isn't that a fine secret of Peter Rabbit's?" exclaimed Sammy, just as if he knew all about it.

Johnny Chuck raised his eyebrows and put on the most surprised look.

"Do tell me what it is!" he begged.

"Oh, if you don't know, I won't tell, for that wouldn't be fair," replied Sammy, and tried to look very honest and innocent, and then he flew over to the Green Forest. And as he flew, he said to himself: "Johnny Chuck can't fool me; he does know Peter Rabbit's secret."

Over in the Green Forest he found Drummer the Woodpecker making a great racket on the hollow

limb of an old chestnut. Sammy sat down near by
and listened. "My, that's fine! I wish I could do that.
You must be practising," said Sammy at the end of
a long rat-a-tat-tat.

Drummer the Woodpecker felt very much flattered. "I am," said he. "I'm practising for Peter Rabbit's party."

"I thought so," replied Sammy Jay. Of course he
hadn't thought anything of the kind.

"Won't Unc' Billy Possum be surprised?"
remarked Drummer the Woodpecker, as he sat
down to rest.

"He surely will," replied Sammy Jay, and then he
flattered and flattered Drummer the Woodpecker
until finally Drummer told all about Peter's plan for
a surprise party for Unc' Billy Possum.

By and by, as he flew home, Sammy Jay chuckled
and said:

"You've got to rise 'fore break of day
   If you want to fool old Mr. Jay."

VII
Four Little Scamps Plan Mischief

"Some folks think they're mighty smart—
    Oh, la me! Oh, la me!
Like the knave who stole the tart—
    Oh, la me! Oh, la me!
Some folks will waken up some day—
And find they can't fool Mr. Jay!"

SAMMY Jay was mightily pleased with himself. He had found out all about Peter Rabbit's plan to give Unc' Billy Possum a surprise party when his family came up from "Ol' Virginny." He had found out that all the little forest and meadow people but himself and his cousin, Blacky the Crow, and Reddy Fox and Shadow the Weasel had been invited, and that each was to bring something good to eat. Sammy Jay smacked his lips as he thought of this. Then he looked up at jolly, round, red Mr. Sun and winked.

Now on all the Green Meadows and in all the Green Forest, there live no greater scamps than Sammy Jay and Blacky the Crow and Reddy Fox and Shadow the Weasel. The worst of it is, they are not honest. They steal whenever they get a chance, and always they try to get others into trouble. That was why Peter Rabbit had left them

out, when he planned his surprise party for Unc'
Billy Possum.

Sammy Jay called the three others together
under the Lone Pine and told them all about Peter
Rabbit's plan and how they had been left out. Of
course Blacky the Crow and Reddy Fox and Shadow the Weasel were angry, very angry indeed, for
no one likes to be left out of a good time. The more
Sammy Jay told them, the angrier they grew;
and the angrier they grew, the more Sammy Jay
chuckled, way down inside. Sammy had a plan, and
the angrier the others grew, the more likely were
they to help him.

"You wait till I catch Peter Rabbit!" said Reddy
Fox and showed all his teeth. He quite forgot that,
despite all his smartness, he never yet had caught
Peter Rabbit.

Blacky the Crow scratched his head thoughtfully. "We can spoil his surprise by telling Unc' Billy
Possum all about it beforehand," said he.

Sammy Jay winked at each of the others. He
cleared his throat and looked all around, to make
sure that no one else was near. Then he leaned for-
ward and whispered: "Let's invite ourselves to the
party."

"What do you mean?" exclaimed the others, all
together.

"Just what I say," replied Sammy. "We'll be the
real surprise. Before the party begins, you will hide
close to where it is to be. When everybody has got

"What do you mean?" exclaimed the others all together.
See page 21.

there and brought all the good things to eat, I'll come flying along and scream: 'Here comes Bowser the Hound!' Of course every one will run away, and we'll have all the good things to eat."

"Haw! haw! haw! The very thing! We'll all be there," cried Blacky the Crow.

The four little scamps shook hands and separated. As they went across the Green Meadows, Sammy Jay's voice floated back to the Lone Pine. He was singing, although he has a very poor voice for singing, and this was his song:

"Some folks think they're mighty smart—
    Oh, la me! Oh, la me!
Like the knave who stole the tart—
    Oh, la me! Oh, la me!
Some folks will waken up some day—
And find they can't fool Mr. Jay!"

"Is that so? Really now, I want to know," said old Mr. Toad, crawling from under the very piece of bark on which Sammy Jay had sat when he told his plan. Then old Mr. Toad winked slowly and solemnly at jolly, round, red Mr. Sun and started off to find Peter Rabbit.

VIII
Peter Rabbit Sends Out Word

IT was a beautiful morning. Everybody said so, and what everybody says is usually so. Peter Rabbit wore the broadest kind of a smile. He hopped and skipped all the way down the Lone Little Path on to the Green Meadows and was waiting there when Old Mother West Wind came down from the Purple Hills and, turning her big bag upside down, tumbled out all her children, the Merry Little Breezes, to play. Peter stopped them before they had a chance to run away. He whispered to each, and each in turn started to dance across the Green Meadows to carry the news that this was the day of Peter Rabbit's surprise party for Unc' Billy Possum, whose family would arrive that very morning from way down in "Ol' Virginny."

Sammy Jay had risen very early that morning. Almost at once his sharp eyes had seen Peter Rabbit sending out the Merry Little Breezes. Sammy's wits are as sharp as his eyes, and you know it is very hard to really fool sharp wits. Right away Sammy had guessed what the Merry Little Breezes were hurrying so for, but he sat and waited and listened. Pretty soon he heard Drummer the Woodpecker start a long rat-a-tat-tat over by Unc' Billy Possum's hollow tree. Then Sammy was sure that this was the day of Peter Rabbit's party. Sammy grinned as he hurried off to find Blacky the Crow and Reddy Fox and Shadow the Weasel.

Reddy was not yet out of bed, but when he heard Sammy Jay at his door, he tumbled out in a hurry. He didn't stop to get any breakfast, because he had planned to get all he could eat at the party. So he hurried over to where the party was to be. Very cautiously he crept up, and when he was quite sure that no one was about, he crawled into a hollow log which was open at one end. There he stretched himself out and made himself as comfortable as he could.

Pretty soon Shadow the Weasel joined Reddy Fox in the hollow log, and they whispered and chuckled while they waited. They knew that Blacky the Crow was safely hidden in the top of a tall pine, where he could see all that went on, and that Sammy Jay was flying about over the Green Meadows and through the Green Forest, pretending that he was attending wholly to his own business, but really watching all the preparations for Peter Rabbit's party.

At the foot of a tree, in the top of which Prickly Porky the Porcupine was eating his breakfast, sat old Mr. Toad, nodding sleepily. Sammy Jay saw him there but, smart as Sammy is, he didn't once suspect innocent-looking old Mr. Toad. You see, he didn't know that old Mr. Toad had overheard all of his plans.

IX
Mr. Toad and Prickly Porky
Put Their Heads Together

SLOWLY Prickly Porky the Porcupine climbed down from the top of the tall poplar tree where he had been getting his breakfast of tender young bark. He grunted as he worked his way down, for he had with him a bundle of bark to take over to Peter Rabbit's surprise party. When he reached the ground, Prickly Porky shook himself until he rattled the thousand little spears hidden in his long coat.

"Tee-hee-hee!"

"Who dares to laugh at me?" demanded Prickly Porky, shaking himself until all the little spears rattled again, and some of them began to peep out of his long coat.

"No one is laughing at you," replied a voice right behind him.

Prickly Porky turned around. There sat old Mr. Toad. His big mouth was stretched wide open, and he was laughing all to himself. Something was tickling old Mr. Toad mightily.

Prickly Porky scowled, and a few more little spears peeped out of his long coat. You know no one likes to be laughed at, and it certainly did look as if old Mr. Toad was laughing at him.

Mr. Toad stopped laughing and hopped a step nearer. "It's a joke," said he, and slowly winked one eye.

"I don't see any joke," said Prickly Porky, and his voice was very fretful.

Mr. Toad hopped a step nearer. "Are you going to Peter Rabbit's party?"

"Of course I am. What a foolish question," replied Prickly Porky.

"To be sure, a very foolish question, a very foolish question, indeed," assented Mr. Toad. "Do you know that Sammy Jay and Blacky the Crow and Reddy Fox and Shadow the Weasel, who have not been invited, are planning to break up the party and then gobble up all the good things to eat?" he continued.

Prickly Porky laid down his bundle of tender young bark and stared at old Mr. Toad. "How do you know?" he demanded.

Old Mr. Toad chuckled deep down in his throat. "I was underneath a piece of bark on which Sammy Jay was sitting when the plan was made. Of course he didn't know I was there, and of course I didn't tell him."

"Of course not," interrupted Prickly Porky, beginning to grin.

"Of course not," continued Mr. Toad, grinning, too. Then he told Prickly Porky all about the plan he had overheard, how Reddy Fox and Shadow the Weasel and Blacky the Crow were to hide near Unc' Billy Possum's hollow tree, and how Sammy Jay was to frighten away everybody else by pretending that Bowser the Hound was coming.

"Have you told Peter Rabbit?" asked Prickly Porky.

"Not yet, but I'm going to, by and by," replied old Mr. Toad. "But first, I want you to help me fool Sammy Jay and Blacky the Crow and Reddy Fox and Shadow the Weasel. Will you?"

"Of course I will if I can, but how can I?" answered Prickly Porky promptly.

Old Mr. Toad hopped up, and stretching up on tiptoe, whispered in one of Prickly Porky's ears. Prickly Porky began to smile. Then he began to chuckle. Finally he laughed until he had to hold his sides.

"Will you do it?" asked Mr. Toad.

Prickly Porky reached for his bundle of tender young bark. "Of course I will," said he, still chuckling. "Come on, Mr. Toad, it's time we were going."

X
The Runaway Cabbage

REDDY Fox, hiding with Shadow the Weasel in a hollow log near Unc' Billy Possum's home, nudged Shadow with his elbow.

"I hear some one coming," he whispered.

Shadow peeped out. "It's old Mr. Toad and Prickly Porky," he whispered back.

Something that sounded very much like a growl sounded way down deep in the throat of Reddy Fox, for Reddy has no love for Prickly Porky.

"And there comes Jimmy Skunk, with a big goose egg under each arm!" continued Shadow, smacking his lips. Reddy Fox wriggled up where he could peep out, too.

"My goodness! What's that coming down the Lone Little Path?" whispered Reddy.

Shadow looked. Then he began to laugh, and Reddy began to laugh, too. But it was laughter that made no sound, for Reddy and Shadow didn't want any one to know that they were hiding there. It was a funny sight they were peeping out at. It certainly was a funny sight. Down the Lone Little Path came Peter Rabbit and his cousin, Jumper the Hare, rolling a huge cabbage.

Right at the top of a little hill the cabbage got

away from them. Down it started, rolling and bounding along, with Peter Rabbit and Jumper the Hare frantically trying to catch it. Just ahead was Johnny Chuck with a big bundle of sweet clover, which he was bringing to Peter Rabbit's party. He didn't see the big cabbage coming. It knocked his feet from under him, and down he went with a thump, flat on his back. Right on top of him fell Jumper the Hare, who was close behind the run-away cabbage and had no time to turn aside. Over the two of them fell Peter Rabbit. Such a mix-up!

And the big cabbage kept right on running away. Jimmy Skunk, who never hurries, heard the noise behind him and turned to see what it all meant. But he didn't have time to more than blink his eyes before the runaway cabbage hit him full in the stomach. Down went Jimmy Skunk with a grunt. One big egg flew over against a tree and broke. Jimmy landed on the other, and this broke, too.

Such a sight as Jimmy Skunk was! Egg dripped from every part of his handsome black and white coat. It was in his eyes and all over his face and dripped from his whiskers. Shadow the Weasel and Reddy Fox, hiding in the hollow log, laughed until the tears rolled down their cheeks, though down in the heart of Shadow was bitter disappointment, for he had planned to steal those very eggs.

Just a little way beyond Jimmy Skunk the run-away cabbage brought up with a thump against a stump on which sat Striped Chipmunk, with the pockets in his cheeks filled full of yellow corn. The sudden bump of the big cabbage made Striped Chipmunk lose his balance, and off he tumbled, right down on to old Mr. Toad, who had just sat down behind the stump for a few minutes of rest. It knocked all the wind out of Mr. Toad, and of course Striped Chipmunk spilled all his corn.

Prickly Porky the Porcupine heard the noise. He looked up to see a strange thing bounding down the Lone Little Path. Prickly Porky didn't wait to see what it was. He did just what he always does when he thinks there may be danger; he rolled himself up with his face hidden in his waistcoat, and when he did that, the thousand little spears hidden in his coat stood out until he looked like a giant chestnut burr.

The runaway cabbage bounced off the stump and hit Prickly Porky. Then it stopped. Where it had touched Prickly Porky, the sharp little spears had stuck into it, so that when Peter Rabbit and Jumper the Hare hurried up, there lay the runaway cabbage, looking for all the world like a great green pincushion.

XI
Reddy Fox Goes Hungry

LIKE a great green pincushion lay the runaway cabbage of Peter Rabbit and Jumper the Hare. Every one thought it was the very best joke ever. Jimmy Skunk had gone off to take a bath and get two more eggs for Peter Rabbit's party. Reddy Fox and Shadow the Weasel, peeping out from the hollow log where they were hiding, could see Jimmy on his way back with a big goose egg under each arm. Shadow smacked his lips. He meant to have those eggs himself.

Pretty soon all the little forest and meadow people whom Peter Rabbit had invited were gathered around the foot of Unc' Billy Possum's hollow tree, and each had brought something good to eat. My, such a feast as was spread out there! Now they were waiting for Unc' Billy Possum, who had gone to meet his family, coming up from "Ol' Virginny."

Over in the top of a tall pine tree Blacky the Crow was hiding and chuckling to himself as he watched. Reddy Fox was getting impatient. He was hungry. He had had no breakfast, and as he lay hiding in the hollow log, he could peep out and see all the good things, and he could smell them, too. It seemed as if his stomach would just give him no peace at all. He wished that Sammy Jay would bring the false message that Bowser the Hound was coming, so as to frighten all the rest away.

"I'm nearly starved!" whispered Reddy Fox. "I hope Sammy Jay will hurry up."

Just then they noticed that Peter Rabbit was very busy. He hopped from guest to guest and whispered in the ear of each.

"Now I wonder what Peter Rabbit is whispering about," said Reddy.

Suddenly the light at the end of the hollow log disappeared. There was a queer rattling sound that sent shivers up and down Reddy's backbone. Prickly Porky the Porcupine had sat down with his back against the end of the hollow log, and the queer rattling sound was made by the thousand little spears in his long coat. Reddy Fox and Shadow the Weasel were in a prison. You see there was no other opening to the hollow log.

"Never mind," whispered Shadow the Weasel, "he'll go away when Sammy Jay shouts that Bowser the Hound is coming."

Blacky the Crow, hidden in the top of the tall pine, was also wondering what Peter was whispering. His sharp eyes watched Peter, and every time that Peter whispered in the ear of one of the little meadow or forest people, they would laugh.

Now, Sammy Jay knew nothing about all this. By and by, when he thought that every one was there, Sammy came flying through the Green Forest, just as if he knew nothing about Peter Rabbit's party. Now, Sammy, with all his faults, is one of the best watchmen in the Green Forest. If there is any danger which his sharp eyes discover, he always screams at the top of his lungs. So, though he steals and plays tricks and makes life very uncomfortable for the others, they always stop to listen when Sammy sounds a warning. Because Sammy knew this he felt sure of breaking up this party.

As soon as he came in sight of all the little meadow and forest people, he began to shriek at the top of his lungs.

"Run! run! run! Here comes Bowser the Hound," he shouted.

No one moved, and this puzzled Sammy so that he hardly knew what to do, but he kept right on shrieking, just as if Bowser was right close at hand. Still no one moved. Sammy stopped on a tall pine and pretended to be terribly excited.

"You had better run before Bowser gets here," he shouted.

What do you think happened then? Why, everybody set up a great shout. "Ha! ha! ha!" laughed Peter Rabbit.

"Ho! ho! ho!" shouted Johnny Chuck.

"Hee! hee! hee!" giggled Danny Meadow Mouse.

"What time will Bowser get here?" asked Bobby Coon, gravely.

"Tell Bowser that we are all waiting for him," added Jimmy Skunk.

"Is Bowser quite out of breath?" inquired Jerry Muskrat.

"I would like nothing better than to run a race with Bowser the Hound," said Jumper the Hare, sitting up very straight.

Sammy Jay didn't know what to do or what to say. He was just the most disgusted looking Jay that ever flew through the Green Forest, and all the time he wondered and wondered and wondered how it could be that Peter Rabbit and his friends knew that Bowser the Hound was not in the Green Forest at all. You see, old Mr. Toad had told Peter all about Sammy's plan, and this is what Peter had been whispering to the others.

XII
Prickly Porky Makes Himself at Home

PETER Rabbit's party promised to be a great success. When old Mr. Toad, who had overheard Sammy Jay's plan, had told Peter Rabbit all about it, he had also told Peter that Reddy Fox and Shadow the Weasel were hiding in an old hollow log close by.

Peter had whispered the news in the ear of each of the little forest and meadow people and had told them how Prickly Porky was even then sitting with his back against the opening in the hollow log.

Every one had thought this the best joke ever, for, of course, they all knew that Reddy Fox and Shadow the Weasel could not get out past the thousand little spears hidden in the long coat of Prickly Porky.

Prickly Porky settled himself very comfortably and began to tell stories about his home, way up in the North Woods. Every few minutes he would rattle the thousand little spears in his coat, and though no one could see Reddy Fox and Shadow the Weasel inside the hollow log, every one could guess just how little shivers were running up and down the backbones of the two little scamps held prisoners there.

Prickly Porky told how in the cold, cold winter the snow piled up and piled up in his far northern home, until nearly all the forest folk who lived there had to make a long journey into the South, or else went into warm, snug hollows in the trees or caves in the rocks and slept the long winter through, just as Johnny Chuck does. He told how the Indians came through the great forest on big webbed shoes, that kept them from sinking into the snow, and hunted for Lightfoot the Deer, and how they never bothered Prickly Porky, but always treated him with the greatest respect. He told so many, many interesting things about the great North Woods, that all the little meadow people and forest folk gathered close around to listen, but every few minutes, while he was talking, he would shake his thousand little spears, and then every one would smile.

Inside the hollow log Reddy Fox was getting stiff and sore, because, you know, he didn't have room enough to even turn over. Worse still, he was so hungry that he could cry. You see, he had crept in there very early in the morning without any breakfast, because he had planned that when Sammy Jay should break up Peter Rabbit's party, he would steal all the good things he wanted. Now, he could smell them, and hear the others talking about the feast they were going to have, and he knew that not so much as a tiny, tiny crumb would be left for him, when Prickly Porky should choose to let him out.

Shadow the Weasel felt just as uncomfortable as Reddy Fox, and Shadow is very short-tempered. Every time Reddy moved and squeezed Shadow, Shadow would snap at him. Now, of course, they could hear everything that was said outside, and the things that were said were not pleasant to listen to. Bobby Coon and Billy Mink and Johnny Chuck and Little Joe Otter and Jimmy Skunk told about all the mean things and all the sharp tricks that Reddy Fox and Shadow had done. It made the two little prisoners so angry that they ground their teeth, but every time they made the least little movement, Prickly Porky would shake his thousand little spears and settle himself still more firmly against the opening in the hollow log. He certainly was enjoying himself. It tickled him almost to pieces to think how easily he had trapped smart Reddy Fox, the boaster.

So they waited all the long day for the coming of Unc' Billy Possum's family, and when at last they did arrive, there was the merriest surprise party ever seen. Only Sammy Jay, Blacky the Crow, Reddy Fox and Shadow the Weasel were unhappy, and of course no one cared for that.

XIII
Unc' Billy Possum Grows Hungry

UNC' Billy Possum spent the very coldest days
of winter curled up in his warm, snug home in
the big hollow tree in the Green Forest. Unc' Billy
didn't like the cold weather. Sometimes he would
stick his head out of his doorway and then, as he
heard rough Brother North Wind whooping
through the Green Forest, he would turn right
around and go back to his bed for another nap.
And all the time he would be saying:

> "Way down Souf de sun am shinin'—
> Yas, Sah, dat am so!
> Fo' dat lan' mah heart am pinin'—
> Yas, Sah, dat am so!
> De mocking-bird he sings all day,
> De alligators am at play,
> De flowers dey am bloomin' fair,
> And mah heart aches to be down there—
> Yas, Sah, dat am so!"

Now Unc' Billy had prepared for the winter by
getting just as fat as he knew how. He was so fat
that he could hardly waddle when Jack Frost first
came to the Green Forest. You see he knew that if
he was very, very fat he wouldn't have to worry

about getting anything to eat, not for a long time, anyway. So when the ice and snow came, and Unc' Billy decided that it was more comfortable indoors than outdoors, he was almost as fat as Johnny Chuck was when he went to sleep for the long winter.

Now Johnny Chuck just slept and slept and slept, without waking once the whole winter long. But Unc' Billy Possum couldn't sleep like that. He had to stick his head out every little while to see how the world was getting along without him. When the sun was bright and the air was not too cold, Unc' Billy would sometimes climb down from his hollow tree and walk about a little on the snow. But he didn't enjoy it much. It made his feet cold, and then he didn't like the tracks he made. He scowled at them, for he knew well enough that if Farmer Brown's boy should happen along, he would know right away who had made those tracks, and then he would hunt for Unc' Billy's home in the hollow tree. So Unc' Billy didn't go out very much, and very seldom indeed when the snow was soft.

It seemed to Unc' Billy Possum as if the winter never, never would go. He was beginning to grow thin now, and of course he was getting hungry. He began to think about it, and the more he thought about it, the hungrier he grew. One morning he stuck his head out of his doorway, and whom should he see trotting along below but Jimmy

Skunk. Jimmy looked fat and comfortable and as if he did not mind the cold weather at all.

"Good mo'ning, Jimmy Skunk," said Unc' Billy.

Jimmy Skunk looked up. "Hello, Unc' Billy!" he exclaimed. "I haven't seen you for a long time!"

"Whar yo' been, Jimmy Skunk?" asked Unc' Billy.

Jimmy winked one eye. "Getting my breakfast of nice fresh eggs," he replied.

Unc' Billy Possum's mouth began to water. "Did yo' leave any?" he anxiously inquired.

Jimmy Skunk allowed that he did, and Unc' Billy gave a long sigh, as he watched Jimmy Skunk amble off up the Lone Little Path. Unc' Billy couldn't sleep any more now. No, Sir, he couldn't sleep a wink. All he could do was to think how hungry he was. He would shut his eyes, and then it seemed as if he could see right into Farmer Brown's hen-house, and there were eggs, eggs, eggs, everywhere. Finally Unc' Billy made up his mind.

"Ah'm going up there the very first dark night!" said he.

XIV
Old Mrs. Possum Grows Worried

OLD Mrs. Possum counted her babies to be sure that they all were tucked snug and warm in their bed in the old hollow tree in the Green Forest. "One, two, three, four, five, six, seven, eight." They were all there. Mrs. Possum looked at them with a great deal of pride and sighed as she thought of how soon they would be leaving the old hollow tree to see the great world and make homes for themselves. Just as soon as the beautiful spring came, they would one by one slip away. Mrs. Possum sighed again. She didn't like winter. No, Sir, she didn't like winter one bit. But when she thought of how her babies would leave her, she almost wished that spring never would come.

Sure that her babies were warm and comfortable, old Mrs. Possum went to the door and looked out. It was plain to be seen that Mrs. Possum was worried. That was the tenth time she had looked out in half an hour. Her sharp little old face looked sharper than ever. It always looks sharper when she is worried, just as the tongues of some people always grow sharper when they are worried.

"Ah don' see what can be keepin' mah ol' man!

Ah'm plumb worried to death," muttered old Mrs. Possum.

Right that very minute she heard a noise outside that made her hurry to the door and thrust her head out once more. It was Sammy Jay, shrieking:

"Thief! Thief! Thief!" at the top of his lungs.

"He's a thief himself and just a low-down mischief-maker, for all his smart clo'es, but he knows a powerful lot about what is going on in the Green Forest, and perhaps he has seen mah ol' man," said old Mrs. Possum, as she tried to make her sharp face as pleasant as possible. She looked over at Sammy Jay, who was in the next tree, and smiled, and when she smiled she showed all her sharp teeth.

"Good mo'ning, Brer Jay," said she.

"Hello!" exclaimed Sammy Jay, not at all politely. "Where's Uncle Billy Possum?"

Old Mrs. Possum shook her head, and the worried look came back into her face, although she tried hard, oh, so hard, not to let it.

"He done go out fo' a walk," replied old Mrs. Possum. "Ah reckons yo'all just got up, or yo' would have met up with him somewhere."

Old Mrs. Possum said this just to try to make Sammy Jay talk, for Sammy is very quick-tempered, and quick-tempered people often say a lot more than they mean to. You see, Mrs. Possum was quite sure that if Sammy Jay knew how worried she was over Unc' Billy Possum, he would

refuse to tell her whether or not he had seen Unc'
Billy, for Sammy Jay is mean and loves to torment
others.

Sammy's temper flared up right away. "I've been
up ever since sun-up!" he sputtered. "Your old man
isn't anywhere in the Green Forest, unless he's
gone to sleep in some other hollow tree, and I
wouldn't blame him a bit if he had! No, Sir, I
wouldn't blame him the least bit!"

"Keep your temper, Brer Jay!
Keep your temper, do, Oh pray!"

said old Mrs. Possum, grinning in the most aggra-
vating way as she turned back to her babies. She
had found out what she wanted to know—Sammy
Jay had seen nothing of Unc' Billy Possum. Old
Mrs. Possum sat down with her head in her hands.
She was more worried than ever.

XV
The Foolishness of Unc' Billy Possum

IF Unc' Billy Possum hadn't happened to look out of his doorway in the big hollow tree in the Green Forest, or if Jimmy Skunk hadn't happened to come along just that very minute, or if Unc' Billy hadn't asked Jimmy where he had been, or if Jimmy hadn't mentioned nice fresh eggs, Unc' Billy wouldn't have been foolish, and old Mrs. Possum wouldn't have been worried. But all those things did happen.

After Jimmy Skunk had mentioned his fine breakfast of fresh eggs, Unc' Billy Possum couldn't think of anything else. He knew well enough where Jimmy had found those eggs. Yes, indeed, Unc' Billy knew all about it. He could shut his eyes and just see the inside of Farmer Brown's hen-house with the rows of hens and roosters sitting on the roosts at one end, their heads tucked under their wings. He could see the rows of nests and the beautiful brown eggs in them. Jimmy Skunk couldn't climb, and so he could have gotten only the eggs in the lowest nests. Now if he, Unc' Billy, had been there, he could have climbed to the very topmost nest and—but what was the use of thinking about it? He hadn't been there, and he couldn't go now, because it was daylight.

All the rest of the day Unc' Billy tried to sleep, but when he did sleep he dreamed about eggs, nice, fresh, delicious eggs, and when he was awake he thought about eggs. It made him more and more uneasy and fidgety. Old Mrs. Possum couldn't stand it.

"What all am the matter with yo'?" she snapped. "Ah do wish yo' would keep still a minute!"

Unc' Billy muttered something, but all that Mrs. Possum could hear was "eggs."

"Now don't yo'all get to thinking of such foolishness as eggs," she commanded. "It isn't safe to be snooping around Farmer Brown's hen-house when there's snow on the ground. Yo' just fo'get all about eggs! Do yo' hear what Ah say?"

Unc' Billy nodded that he did. But just the same he couldn't think of anything else. He knew that old Mrs. Possum was right, and that it wasn't safe to go fooling around Farmer Brown's hen-house and leaving his tracks for everybody who came along to see. Just the same, Unc' Billy felt that he had got to have a nice fresh egg. He had *got* to have it. That is all there was about it.

As soon as jolly, round, red Mr. Sun had gone to bed behind the Purple Hills that night, Unc' Billy crept out of his home in the hollow tree.

"Where are yo' going?" demanded Mrs. Possum.

"Just to stretch the kinks out of mah legs," replied Unc' Billy.

Old Mrs. Possum looked after him suspiciously. "Don't yo' go fo' to do any foolishness!" she called.

Unc' Billy didn't answer. He was on his way to Farmer Brown's hen-house.

XVI
Why Unc' Billy Possum Didn't Go Home

UNC' Billy Possum had a very good reason for not going home, a very good reason, indeed. Even old Mrs. Possum would have thought it was a good reason, could she have known it. But she didn't know it, and so she sat in the home in the big hollow tree in the Green Forest and worried herself almost sick, because Unc' Billy didn't come home, and she didn't know what might have happened to him.

Sometimes Unc' Billy wished that he was back in the old hollow tree, and sometimes he was glad that he was right where he was. Sometimes he felt little shivers of fear run all over him as he thought of what might become of him if he should be found. Sometimes a little tickly feeling of pleasure ran all over him, as he bit a hole in the end of a freshly laid egg and sucked the egg out of the shell.

Now Unc' Billy was very, very crafty. He had found Jimmy Skunk's tracks boldly leading up to the hen-house, so Unc' Billy had stepped as carefully as he knew how in the footprints of Jimmy Skunk, in order that Farmer Brown's boy might think that Jimmy Skunk was the only visitor to the hen-house. But with all his craft, there was one

thing that Unc' Billy forgot. Yes, Sir, there was one
thing Unc' Billy forgot all about. He forgot to keep
his tail up. He was trying so hard to step in the
footprints of Jimmy Skunk, that he forgot all about
that little, smooth, handy old tail of his, and he let
it drag along the snow.

When Unc' Billy was safely in the hen-house, he
hurried from one nest to another. There were eggs,
plenty of them. It seemed to him that nothing he
had ever seen before had looked half so good as
those eggs. He just ate and ate and ate until he
couldn't eat another one. Now a full stomach is
very apt to make a sleepy head. Unc' Billy knew
that the thing for him to do was to hurry home as
fast as he could go, but he didn't. No, Sir, he didn't
do it. The hen-house was warm and here were
some of the nicest nests of hay. He was tired after
his long walk from the Green Forest, for Unc' Billy
had done so little walking this winter that he was
rather out of practice. Why not take a teeny, weeny
nap before he started back home?

Unc' Billy climbed to the very last nest in the
topmost row, way up in a dark corner. It hadn't
been used for a long time, but it was full of nice,
soft hay. Unc' Billy curled himself up in it, and with
a great sigh of contentment, closed his eyes for
that teeny, weeny nap. He didn't open them again
until he heard an angry voice right close to him. He
peeped out. It was broad daylight, and there, just
below him, was Farmer Brown's boy, looking at the

He just ate and ate and ate until
he couldn't eat another one. *See page 49*.

empty egg-shells left by Unc' Billy. Farmer Brown's boy was angry. Yes, indeed, he was very, very angry. Unc' Billy shivered as he listened. Then he snuggled down out of sight under the hay of the nest.

XVII
Unc' Billy Possum Lies Low

FARMER Brown's boy was angry. Yes, Sir, he was angry. There was no doubt about that. He had found the empty shells of the eggs which Unc' Billy had eaten in the night, and Unc' Billy knew by the sound of his voice that Farmer Brown's boy meant to find the thief.

It was a terrible position to be in, right there in the hen-house, with no chance to run. Unc' Billy wished with all his might that he had never thought of eggs, and that he was safe back home in the dear old hollow tree in the Green Forest. Oh, dear! oh, dear! Why hadn't he gone right straight back there, after eating those eggs, instead of taking a nap? But he hadn't. He had taken a nap and overslept, and here he was, right in the hen-house, in broad daylight.

"It must have been a Skunk," said Farmer Brown's boy, "and if it was, he must have left some tracks in the snow outside. I'll just look around a bit."

Unc' Billy almost chuckled as he heard Farmer Brown's boy go out.

"He'll find Jimmy Skunk's tracks, but he won't find mine," thought Unc' Billy. "Isn't it lucky that I thought to step right in Jimmy Skunk's tracks when I came here?"

He lay still and listened to Farmer Brown's boy poking around outside. He heard him exclaim: "Ah, I thought so!" and knew that he had found the tracks Jimmy Skunk had made in the snow. Unc' Billy almost chuckled again as he thought what a smart fellow he had been to step in Jimmy Skunk's tracks. And right then he heard something that put an end to all his fine thoughts about his own smartness, and sent little cold shivers up and down his backbone.

"Hello!" said the voice of Farmer Brown's boy. "These are queer tracks! That Skunk must have had a queer tail, for here are the marks of it in the snow, and they look as if they might have been made by the tail of a very big rat."

Unc' Billy remembered then for the first time that when he had thought he was so smart, he had forgotten to hold his tail up. He had dragged it in the snow, and of course it had left a mark.

"I guess that there was more than one visitor here last night," continued the voice of Farmer Brown's boy. "Here are the tracks of the Skunk going away from the hen-house, but I don't see any of those other queer tracks going away. Whoever made them must be right around here now."

Back into the hen-house came Farmer Brown's boy and began to poke around in all the corners. He moved all the boxes and looked in the grain bin.

Then he began to look in the nests. Unc' Billy could hear him coming nearer and nearer. He was looking in the very next nest to the one in which Unc' Billy was. Finally he looked into that very nest. Unc' Billy Possum held his breath.

Now the nest in which Unc' Billy was hiding was on the topmost row in the darkest corner of the hen-house, and Unc' Billy had crawled down underneath the hay. Perhaps it was because that corner was so dark, or perhaps it was because that nest was so high up, that Farmer Brown's boy really didn't expect to find anything there. Anyway, all he saw was the hay, and he didn't take the trouble to put his hand in and feel for anything under the hay.

"It's queer," said Farmer Brown's boy. "It's very queer! I guess I shall have to set some traps."

And all the time Unc' Billy Possum held his breath and lay low.

XVIII
Unc' Billy Possum Is a Prisoner

"Mah home is in a holler tree—
    It's a long way home!
Ah wish Ah's there, but here Ah be—
    It's a long way home!
If Ah had only been content
Instead of out on mischief bent,
Ah'd have no reason to repent—
    It's a long way home!"

UNC' Billy Possum lay curled up under the hay in the highest nest in the darkest corner in Farmer Brown's hen-house. Unc' Billy didn't dare go to sleep, because he was afraid that Farmer Brown's boy might find him. And, anyway, he wanted to see just what Farmer Brown's boy was doing. So peeping out, he watched Farmer Brown's boy, who seemed to be very busy indeed. What do you think he was doing? Unc' Billy knew. Yes, Sir, Unc' Billy knew just what Farmer Brown's boy was doing. He was setting traps.

Unc' Billy's eyes twinkled as he watched Farmer Brown's boy, for Unc' Billy knew that those traps were being set for him, and now that he knew just where each one was, of course he wasn't a bit afraid. It seemed to Unc' Billy that it was just the greatest kind of a joke to be watching Farmer Brown's boy set those traps, while all the time Farmer Brown's boy thought he was hiding them so cleverly that the only way they would be found would be by some one stepping into one and getting caught.

"There," said Farmer Brown's boy, as he set the last trap, "I'd like to see anything get into this hen-house now without getting caught!"

Unc' Billy almost chuckled aloud. Yes, Sir, he almost chuckled aloud. It was such a funny idea that Farmer Brown's boy should have taken all the trouble to set those traps to catch Unc' Billy trying to get into the hen-house, when all the time he was already in there.

Unc' Billy laughed under his breath as Farmer Brown's boy closed the door of the hen-house and went off whistling. "Ho, ho, ho! Ha, ha, ha! Hee, hee!" Unc' Billy broke off short, right in the very middle of his laugh. He had just thought of something, and it wasn't funny at all. With all those traps set at every opening to the hen-house, no one could get in without getting caught, and of course no one who was in could get out without getting caught!

The joke wasn't on Farmer Brown's boy, after all; it was on Unc' Billy Possum. But Unc' Billy couldn't see that it was any joke at all. Unc' Billy was a prisoner, a prisoner in Farmer Brown's hen-house, and he didn't know how ever he was going to get out of there.

It's a long way home," said Unc' Billy mournfully, as he peeped out of a crack toward the Green Forest.

XIX
What the Snow Did

UNC' Billy Possum did a lot of thinking. He was a prisoner, just as much a prisoner as if he were in a cage. Now Unc' Billy Possum wouldn't have minded being a prisoner in the hen-house but for two things; he was dreadfully afraid that his old friend and partner, Jimmy Skunk, would get hungry for eggs and would get caught in the traps, and he was still more afraid that Farmer Brown's boy would think to put his hand down under the hay in the last nest of the top row in the darkest corner. So Unc' Billy spent most of his time studying and thinking of some way to get out, and if he couldn't do that, of some way to warn Jimmy Skunk to keep away from Farmer Brown's hen-house.

If it hadn't been for those two worries, Unc' Billy would have been willing to stay there the rest of the winter. It was delightfully warm and cosy. He knew which nest Mrs. Speckles always used and which one Mrs. Feathertoes liked best, and he knew that of all the eggs laid in Farmer Brown's hen-house those laid by Mrs. Speckles and Mrs. Feathertoes were the best. Having all the eggs he could eat, Unc' Billy had grown very particular. Nothing but the best, the very best, would do for

58

him. So he would lie curled up in the last nest of the top row in the darkest corner and wait until he heard the high-pitched voice of Mrs. Speckles proudly crying:

"Cut, cut, cut, cut, cut, cut-aa-cut! I lay the finest eggs in the world!"

Then Unc' Billy would chuckle to himself and wait a few minutes longer for the voice of Mrs. Feathertoes, saying: "Cut, cut, cut, cut, cut-aa-cut, cut, cut, cut! No one lays such splendid eggs as I do!" Then, while Mrs. Speckles and Mrs. Feathertoes were disputing as to which laid the best eggs, Unc' Billy would slip out and breakfast on both those newly laid eggs.

So for almost a week Unc' Billy lived in Farmer Brown's hen-house and ate the eggs of Mrs. Speckles and Mrs. Feathertoes and hid in the last nest of the top row in the darkest corner and shivered as he heard Farmer Brown's boy tell what would happen if he caught the one who was stealing those eggs. Sometimes the door was left open during the day, and Unc' Billy would peep out and wish that he dared to run. But he didn't, for Bowser the Hound was always prowling around, and then again he was almost sure to be seen by some one.

At last one day it began to snow. It snowed all day and it snowed all night. Rough Brother North Wind piled it up in great drifts in front of the hen-house door and all along one side of the hen-house. It covered the traps so deep that they couldn't possibly catch any one. As soon as the snow stopped falling, Unc' Billy began to dig his way up to the top from the very hole by which he had entered the hen-house. He didn't like it, for he doesn't like snow, but now was his chance to get away, and he meant to make the most of it.

XX
Unc' Billy Possum Wishes He Had Snowshoes

UNC' Billy Possum didn't know whether he liked
the snow more than he hated it or hated it
more than he liked it, just now. Usually he dislikes
the snow very much, and doesn't go out in it any
more than he has to. But this time the snow had
done Unc' Billy a good turn, a very good turn,
indeed. Once out of the hen-house, Unc' Billy lost
no time in starting for the Green Forest. But it was
slow, hard work. You see, the snow was newly fall-
en and very soft. Of course Unc' Billy sank into it
almost up to his middle at every step. He huffed
and he puffed and he grunted and groaned. You
see Unc' Billy had slept so much through the winter that he was not at all used to hard work of any
kind, and he wasn't half way to the Green Forest
before he was so tired it seemed to him that he
could hardly move, and so out of breath that he
could only gasp. It was then that he was sure that
he hated the snow more than he liked it, even if it
had set him free from the hen-house of Farmer
Brown.

Now it never does to let one's wits go to sleep.
Some folks call it forgetting, but forgetting is nothing but sleepy wits. And sleepy wits get more

61

people into trouble than anything else in the world. Unc' Billy Possum's wits were asleep when he left Farmer Brown's hen-house. If they hadn't been, he would have remembered this little saying:

> The wits that live within my head
> Must never, never go to sleep,
> For if they should I might forget
> And Trouble on me swiftly leap.

But Unc' Billy's wits certainly were asleep. He was so tickled over the idea that he could get out of the hen-house, that he couldn't think of anything else, and so he forgot. Yes, Sir, Unc' Billy forgot! What did he forget? Why, he forgot that that nice, soft snow, which so kindly buried the dreadful traps so that they could do no harm, couldn't be waded through without leaving tracks. Unc' Billy forgot all about that, until he was half way to the Green Forest, and then, as he sat down to rest and get his breath, he remembered.

Unc' Billy looked behind him, and he turned pale. Yes, Sir, Unc' Billy Possum turned pale! There, all the way from Farmer Brown's hen-house, was a broad trail in the smooth white snow, where he had plowed his way through. If Farmer Brown's boy should come out to look at his traps, he would see that track at once, and all he would have to do would be to follow it until it led him to Unc' Billy.

"Oh, dear! Oh, dear! Whatever did Ah leave the hen-house for?" wailed Unc' Billy.

There, all the way from Farmer Brown's hen-house, was
a broad trail in the smooth white snow. *See page 62.*

His wits were all wide awake now. It wouldn't do to go back. Farmer Brown's boy would see that he had gone back, and then he would hunt that hen-house through until he found Unc' Billy. No, there was nothing to do but to go on, and trust that Farmer Brown's boy was so snowed in and would be kept so busy shovelling out paths, that he would forget all about looking at his traps. Unc' Billy drew a long breath and began to wade ahead toward the Green Forest.

"If Ah only had snowshoes!" he panted. "If Ah only had snowshoes like Mrs. Grouse."

XXI
Farmer Brown's Boy Chops Down a Tree

"There was an old Possum lived up in a tree;
    Hi, ho, see the chips fly!
The sliest old thief that you ever did see;
    Hi, ho, see the chips fly!
He ate and he ate in the dark of the night,
And when the day came not an egg was in sight,
But now that I know where he's making his bed,
I'll do without eggs and will eat him instead!
    Hi, ho, see the chips fly!"

FARMER Brown's boy sang as he swung his keen axe, and the chips did fly. They flew out on the white snow in all directions. And the louder Farmer Brown's boy sang, the faster the chips flew. Farmer Brown's boy had come to the Green Forest bright and early that morning, and he had made up his mind that he would take home a fat Possum for dinner. He didn't have the least doubt about it, and that is why he sang as he made the chips fly. He had tracked that Possum right up to that tree, and there were no tracks going away from it. Right up near the top he could see a hollow, just such a hollow as a Possum likes. All he had to do was to cut the tree down and split it open, and Mr. Possum would be his.

So Farmer Brown's boy swung his axe, chop, chop, chop, and the chips flew out on the white snow, and Farmer Brown's boy sang, never once thinking of how the Possum he was after might feel. Of course it was Unc' Billy Possum whose tracks he had followed. He had seen them outside of the hen-house, just as Unc' Billy had been afraid that he would. He couldn't very well have helped it, those tracks were so very plain to be seen.

That had been a long, hard, anxious journey for Unc' Billy from Farmer Brown's hen-house to the Green Forest. The snow was so deep that he could hardly wade through it. When he reached that hollow tree, he was so tired that it was all he could do to climb it. Of course it wasn't his own hollow tree, where old Mrs. Possum and the eight little Possums lived. He knew better than to go there, leaving a plain track for Farmer Brown's boy to follow. So he had been very thankful to climb up this hollow tree. And, just as he had feared, there was Farmer Brown's boy.

Chop, chop, chop! The snow was covered with chips now. Chop, chop, chop! The tree began to shiver and then to shake. Cra-a-ck! With a great crash over it went!

Bowser the Hound barked excitedly, and with Farmer Brown's boy rushed to the hollow near the top to catch Mr. Possum, if he should run out. But he didn't run out. Farmer Brown's boy rapped on the tree with the handle of his axe, but no one ran out.

"I guess he's playing dead," said Farmer Brown's boy, and began to split open the tree, so as to get into the hollow. And as he chopped, he began to sing again. Pretty soon he had split the tree wide open. In the bottom of the hollow was an old nest of Chatterer the Red Squirrel, and that was all. Farmer Brown's boy rubbed his eyes and stared and stared and stared. There were Unc' Billy's tracks leading straight up to that tree and none leading away. Did that Possum have wings?

XXII
Where Unc' Billy Possum Was

WHERE was Unc' Billy Possum? That is what Farmer Brown's boy wanted to know. That is what Bowser the Hound wanted to know. Where was Unc' Billy Possum? He was in another hollow tree all the time and laughing till his sides ached as he peeped out and saw how hard Farmer Brown's boy worked.

"Ah done fool him that time," said Unc' Billy, as he watched Farmer Brown's boy wading off home through the snow, with Bowser the Hound at his heels.

"You certainly did, Unc' Billy! How did you do it?" asked a voice right over Unc' Billy's head.

Unc' Billy looked up in surprise. There was Tommy Tit the Chickadee. Unc' Billy grinned.

"Ah just naturally expected Ah was gwine to have visitors, and so Ah prepared a little surprise. Yes, Sah, Ah done prepare a little surprise. Yo' see, mah tracks in the snow was powerful plain. Yes, Sah, they sho'ly was! When Ah had climbed up that tree and looked down and saw all those tracks what Ah done made, Ah began to get powerful anxious. Yes, Sah, Ah done get so anxious Ah just couldn't get any rest in mah mind. Ah knew Farmer

Brown's boy was gwine to find those tracks, and
when he did, he was gwine to follow 'em right
smart quick. Sho' enough, just before sundown,
here he comes. He followed mah tracks right up to
the foot of the tree whar Ah was hiding in the hollow, and Ah heard him say:

"So this is whar yo' live, is it, Mistah Possum? Ah
reckon Bowser and Ah'll make yo' a call to-
morrow."

"When I heard him say that, Ah felt right bad.
Yes, Sah, Ah sho'ly did feel right smart bad. Ah
studied and Ah studied how Ah was gwine to fool
Farmer Brown's boy and Bowser the Hound. If Ah
climbed down and went somewhere else, Ah would
have to leave tracks, and that boy done bound to
find me just the same. Ah done wish Ah had wings
like yo' and Brer Buzzard.

"So po' ol' Unc' Billy sat studying and studying
and getting mo' and mo' troubled in his mind. By
and by Ah noticed that a branch from that holler
tree rubbed against a branch of another tree, and
a branch of that tree rubbed against a branch of
another tree, and if Ah made a right smart jump
from that tree Ah could get into this tree, which
had a holler just made fo' me. Ah didn't waste no
mo' time studying. No, Sah, Ah just moved right
away, and here Ah am."

"And you didn't leave any tracks, and you didn't
have any wings," said Tommy Tit the Chickadee.

"No," said Unc' Billy, "but Ah done find that yo'

can most always find a way out, if yo' look hard
enough. Just now, Ah am looking right smart hard
fo' a way to get home, but Ah reckon mah eyesight
am failing; Ah don' see any yet."

"Dee, dee, dee!" laughed Tommy Tit merrily. "Be
patient, Unc' Billy, and perhaps you will."

XXIII
Happy Jack Squirrel
Makes an Unexpected Call

HAPPY Jack Squirrel likes the snow. He always has liked the snow. It makes him feel frisky. He likes to run and jump in it and dig little holes in it after nuts, which he hid under the leaves before the snow fell. When his feet get cold, all he has to do is to scamper up a tree and warm them in his own fur coat. So the big snowstorm which made so much trouble for Unc' Billy Possum just suited Happy Jack Squirrel, and he had a whole lot of fun making his funny little tracks all through that part of the Green Forest in which he lives.

Happy Jack didn't know anything about Unc' Billy Possum's troubles. He supposed that Unc' Billy was safe at home in his own big hollow tree, fast asleep, as he had been most of the winter. Happy Jack couldn't understand how anybody could want to sleep in such fine weather, but that was their own business, and Happy Jack had learned a long time ago not to worry about other people's business.

After frisking about he would stop to rest. Then he would sit up very straight and fold his hands across his breast, where they would get nice and warm in the fur of his coat. His beautiful, great gray tail would be arched up over his back. His bright eyes would snap and twinkle, and then he would shout just for joy, and every time he shouted he jerked his big tail. Farmer Brown's boy called it barking, but it was Happy Jack's way of shouting.

> "I love to romp! I love to play!
> I'm happy, happy, all the day!
> I love the snow, so soft and white!
> I love the sun that shines so bright!
> I love the whole world, for, you see,
> The world is very good to me!"

By and by Happy Jack came to the hollow tree that Farmer Brown's boy had cut down because he thought that Unc' Billy Possum was inside of it.

"Hello!" exclaimed Happy Jack. "That's one of the old storehouses of my cousin, Chatterer the Red Squirrel! I've got an old storehouse near here, and I guess I'll see if I have left any nuts in it."

He scampered over to another hollow tree standing near. He scampered up the tree as only Happy Jack can and whisked in at the open doorway of the hollow. Now Happy Jack had been in that hollow tree so often that he didn't once think of looking to see where he was going, and he landed plump on something that was soft and warm! Happy Jack was so surprised that he didn't know what to do for a second. And then all in a flash that something soft and warm was full of sharp claws and sharper teeth, and an angry growling filled the hollow tree.

Happy Jack was so frightened that he scrambled out as fast as he could. When he was safely outside, he grew very angry to think that any one should be in his storehouse, even if it was an old one. He could hear a very angry voice inside, and in a minute who should appear at the doorway but Unc' Billy Possum.

Unc' Billy had been waked out of a sound sleep, and that was enough to make any one cross. Besides, he had been badly frightened, and that made him crosser still.

"What do yo' mean by trying to frighten honest people?" snapped Unc' Billy, when he caught sight of Happy Jack.

"What do you mean by stealing into other folk's houses?" demanded Happy Jack, just as angrily.

XXIV
Happy Jack Squirrel Helps Unc' Billy Possum

IT is very startling, very startling indeed, to rush into your own storehouse, which you had supposed was empty, and run right into some one sleeping there as if he owned it. It is enough to make any one lose his temper. Happy Jack Squirrel lost his.

And it is very startling, very startling, indeed, to be wakened out of pleasant dreams of warm summer days by having some one suddenly jump on you. It is enough to make any one lose his temper. Unc' Billy Possum lost his.

So Happy Jack sat outside on a branch of the hollow tree where his old storehouse was and scolded, and called Unc' Billy Possum names, and jerked his tail angrily with every word he said. And Unc' Billy Possum sat in the doorway of the hollow tree and showed his teeth to Happy Jack and said unpleasant things. It really was very dreadful the way those two did talk.

But Unc' Billy Possum is really very good-natured, and when he had gotten over the fright Happy Jack had given him and began to understand that he was in one of Happy Jack's storehouses, all his temper vanished, and presently he began to grin and then to laugh. Now it always takes two to make a quarrel, and one of the hardest things in the world is to keep cross when the one you are cross with won't keep cross, too. Happy Jack tried hard to stay angry, but every time he looked at Unc' Billy Possum's twinkling eyes and broad grin, Happy Jack lost a little of his own temper. Pretty soon he was laughing just as hard as Unc' Billy Possum.

"Ho, ho, ho! Ha, ha, ha!" they laughed together. Finally they had to stop for breath.

"What are you doing in my storehouse, Unc' Billy?" asked Happy Jack, when he could stop laughing.

Then Unc' Billy told him all about how he had climbed there from another tree, so as to leave no tracks in the snow for Farmer Brown's boy to follow.

"But now Ah want to go to mah own home in the big hollow tree way down in the Green Forest, but Ah can't, on account of mah tracks in the snow," concluded Unc' Billy mournfully.

Happy Jack put his head on one side and thought very hard. "Why don't you stay right here until the snow goes, Unc' Billy?" he asked.

"Because Ah 'spects that mah ol' woman am worried most to death," said Unc' Billy, in a mournful voice. "Besides," he added, "Ah just done found out that this right nice lil' house belongs to one of mah neighbors." There was a twinkle in Unc' Billy's eyes.

Happy Jack laughed. "You're welcome to stay as long as you like, Unc' Billy," he said. "You better stay right where you are, and I'll go tell old Mrs. Possum where you are."

"Thank yo'! Thank yo'! That is very kind of yo', Brer Squirrel. That will be a great help, fo' it will lift a great load off mah mind," said Unc' Billy.

"Don't mention it, Unc' Billy!" replied Happy Jack and started off with the message to old Mrs. Possum, and as he scampered through the snow he said:

"To get yourself in trouble is a very easy thing.
I notice that to others it will always worries bring.
But getting out of trouble's always quite the other way—
The more you try to wriggle out, the longer you must stay."

XXV
Happy Jack Squirrel's Bright Idea

HAPPY Jack Squirrel frisked along through the snow on his way to Unc' Billy Possum's house in the big hollow tree in the Green Forest to tell old Mrs. Possum that Unc' Billy was safe in another hollow tree on the edge of the Green Forest, but that he didn't dare to come home because he would leave tracks in the snow. He found old Mrs. Possum very much worried and very much out of sorts. You see Unc' Billy had been gone a long time for him, and she didn't know what had become of him.

Now of course old Mrs. Possum was very much relieved when she heard that Unc' Billy was safe, for she had been afraid that something dreadful had happened to him. But just as soon as she knew that he was safe, she forgot all about how worried she had been. All she thought of was how Unc' Billy had gone to get some fresh eggs to put in his own stomach and left her to take care of herself and eight baby Possums.

"Yo' tell Unc' Billy Possum that Ah don' care if he never comes back. Ah done got other things to bother about more'n a worthless, no'count Possum what don' take care of his fam'ly," she said crossly, and hurried into the house to see that the

77

"Yo' tell Unc' Billy Possum that Ah don' care
if he never comes back." *See page 77.*

eight little Possums were properly tucked in bed, for it was a cold day, and the eight little Possums had to stay in bed to keep warm.

Happy Jack chuckled as he started back to tell Unc' Billy Possum. He knew perfectly well that old Mrs. Possum didn't mean what she said. He knew that Unc' Billy would know that she didn't mean it. But he knew, and he knew that Unc' Billy knew, that when he did get home, he would get a great scolding. Then all of a sudden Happy Jack thought of a way for Unc' Billy to get home without waiting until the snow melted away. That might be a very long time, for there was a great deal of snow on the ground.

What do you suppose gave Happy Jack his idea? Why, a tiny little snowflake that hit Happy Jack right on the end of his nose! Yes, Sir, it was that tiny little snowflake that gave Happy Jack Squirrel his bright idea.

He hurried back to the hollow tree where Unc' Billy was hiding and scrambled up to the doorway.

"Hello, Unc' Billy! You can go home to-night!" he shouted.

Unc' Billy Possum stuck his head out of the doorway. "What's that yo' say, Brer Squirrel?" he said. "Ah don' see as the snow has gone away, and your tracks are powerful plain to see, and Ah makes bigger tracks than yo', Brer Squirrel."

"Just look up in the sky, Unc' Billy!" said Happy Jack.

Unc' Billy looked. The sky was full of dancing snowflakes. They got in his eyes and clung to his whiskers. Unc' Billy shook his head in disgust.

"Ah don' see anything but mo snow, and yo' know Ah don' like snow!" he said. "What yo' driving at, Brer Squirrel?"

Happy Jack laughed. "Why, it's just as simple as can be, Unc' Billy!" he cried. "Just as soon as it's dark, you start for home. It's going to snow all night, and in the morning there won't be any tracks. The snowflakes will have covered them all up."

Unc' Billy grinned. "Ah believe yo' are right, Brer Squirrel, Ah believe yo' are right!" said Unc' Billy.

And Happy Jack was right, for Unc' Billy got safely home that very night, and the next morning, when Farmer Brown's boy visited the Green Forest, there wasn't a footprint to be seen anywhere.

So Unc' Billy Possum learned how easy it is to get into trouble and how hard to get out of it. But he isn't the only one who has found this out. Just ask Unc' Billy's particular friend, Mistah Mocker the Mocking Bird. He will tell you the very same thing. He and Unc' Billy have been in all kinds of scrapes together, and if you care to read about some of them, you may do so in the next book—The Adventures of Mistah Mocker.

Write Your Own
Realistic Fiction
Stories

Tish Farrell

Your writing quest

Do you want to tell exciting real-life stories? Is your creative mind transfixed by the emotional problems we all sometimes face? Would you like to write truthfully and accurately about what you see around you? This book will help you to write gripping realistic-fiction stories.

Your mission is to find your own believable realistic-fiction stories to tell. To help you on your way, there will be all kinds of brainstorming exercises and writer's tips that will develop your creative writing skills. There will be hints from famous writers and examples from their books to inspire you.

But don't forget! Becoming a good writer takes lots of time and practice. There are no short cuts to reach your goal.

Now, get ready for the exciting writing quest...

Bon voyage!

Copyright © ticktock Entertainment Ltd 2006
First published in Great Britain in 2006 by ticktock Media Ltd.,
Unit 2, Orchard Business Centre, North Farm Road, Tunbridge Wells, Kent, TN2 3XF
We would like to thank: Starry Dog Books Limited for their help with this book.
ISBN 1 86007 926 1 PB
Printed in China
A CIP catalogue record for this book is available from the British Library.